The Train Wreck

The Living History Series

By

Roddy Huder

Forward

The transcontinental railroad was completed in 1869 when the Union Pacific and the Central Pacific railroads met in Promontory, Utah. As the railroads grew they transformed America. They brought people west who turned the prairies into farms. Cities grew around the railroads as people and goods poured westward. By the 1880's it was the center of American life from coast to coast.

The railroad provided jobs for thousands of people. There were engineers, firemen, the conductors, the brakemen, the surveyors, and station agents to just to name a few. They were all railroad men. It was a way of life those men and their families.

It was also one of the most dangerous jobs in America. Much has been written about cowboys and their adventures but little has been written about the railroad men. They faced all kinds of danger every day. There were blizzards in the winter and tornados in the summer. There were attacks by Indians defending their lands. They fought off bandits and robbers. Bridges crumbled and floods washed out rails. So railroad men faced danger everyday. This is the story of a boy who wanted to be a railroad man.

Table of Content

Chapter 1

Scraeeechhhhh!

It was the most frightening sound Connor Galway had ever heard. It was the sound of metal tearing. It sounded like some great mechanical animal in pain. The railroad passenger car looked normal in the yellow kerosene lamplight.

The carved wooden curlicues on the walls and the bright blue upholstered seats appeared just as they had when the train left the station. The potbellied wood stove with silver rails and glass door sat in the corner of the car as usual.

He looked at the passengers seated in the car. They too had heard it because they all begun to look at each other. The traveling salesman in the bowler hat and the tall tough looking man with a long scar down his face looked around the car. The pretty young woman sitting with her daughter clutched her hand. The older woman in the big hat with an ostrich feather that seemed to take up half of her side of the car turned her head toward the noise. They all had looks of surprise and concern on their faces. The salesman in the bowler hat started to say.

"What..."

That is when Connor felt a tremendous jolt as

the car suddenly jumped off the rails. Then the car tilted violently to the right. Connor was thrown into the air as the car tilted further and further.

Crack!

The sound of wood splintering filled the car.

Boom!

The car tilted more and the passengers and their luggage in the overhead shelf flew into the air. Now he knew what had happened. This is what a train wreck felt and sounded like.

Scrape!

Smash!

The front of the car left the tracks and crashed into the ground. Connor flew through the air toward the other side of the car. He watched as grass appeared in the windows as the car tilted even further. The car rammed into something as he landed on the opposite side of the car between the seats. Dust and debris sprayed Connor through an open window as the car plowed through the dirt. A female passenger screamed as the car continued to skid along the ground.

Snap! Crunch!

It was the sound of the cars wooden walls snapping and splintering, they were being torn apart by the crash. The sound seemed to be coming closer as the passenger car smashed into the baggage car in front of it.

Suddenly there was another tremendous jolt. Connor was thrown up in the air again. He saw the front of the car buckle as the metal platform of the baggage car smashed into their car as the two collided. Their car's front wall buckled inward sending splinters of wood flying through the air. He ducked as a splinter as large as his arm stuck into the back the seat just above his head.

The sounds of the wreck continued as the two cars slid along the ground smashing into one another. The car was on its side so the seats that had been on the left side of the car were now above Connor. Another tremendous jolt slammed Connor down hard.

Creak!

Connor looked up, the seat directly above him was swinging from its bolts.

Screech!

The bolts gave and the seat fell toward Connor.

He curled up in a ball trying to keep from getting hit by the seat. It landed on top of him but most the weight landed on the seats in front and behind him. One of the mental supports fell on his left leg. Connor groaned in pain as the metal support pinned his leg to the floor.

Then as suddenly as it had started the sound stopped. Connor lay there waiting for another impact afraid to move. Everything was strangely quite. There was only the creaking of the newly crushed timber and the sound of luggage finally coming to rest. Connor started to raise his head when he heard the groaning of metal from behind him.

Screech! Snap!

He glanced back and saw the stove slowly swing from its metal legs. It was hanging above him now. Then the iron legs broke free and the stove crashed down to his side of the car.

Crash! Smash!

The door to the stove burst open spreading red-hot coals and burning wood onto the upholstered passenger seats. The seat immediately burst into flames.

Frantically Connor struggled to free his leg. He couldn't free it. He was trapped. The fire was growing by the second. He was trapped in a

passenger train car that was on fire!

Chapter 2

Kanas City, Kanas

Union Pacific Rail yards

8 Hours Earlier

1886

Connor came running into the shanty that his

family now called home. It was made of lumber

found around the train yards with a single door

that led into the one room house. It is where he and his mother Kathleen and little sister Bridget spent their days. Before his father had died of the fever two years ago they had lived in a nice house with bedrooms and even a kitchen. But when his father died there was no money.

His mother began to take in washing from the trainmen and was a cook at a boarding house when they needed extra help. Yet it wasn't enough to provide the kind of life they had been used too. The shanty was the best they could afford.

His father had moved them out west to get a good job and save his money. He was a smart educated man who had worked in the railroad's telegraph office. He had learned to be a telegraph operator during the Civil War.

He saved every dime he could so he could buy land and a wagon to move further west and start his own farm but that dream had come crashing down when he died. Now it was up to Connor and his mother to provide for the three of them.

He had been hired as a callboy for the railroad. When the station agent needed to put together a crew quickly it was up to Connor to race into town and find them. He would hunt through the bars, boarding houses and anywhere else he could find the men to crew the train. These men did not always want to be found.

Many had just gotten off an eighteen or even a twenty-four-hour trip. They wanted nothing more than to eat, drink and sleep not to go back out on a run. So it was not always easy to locate the men needed for a crew. Connor had become good at finding the men and the station-agent had taken notice. The money he made as a callboy was not nearly enough to help his mother and sister but now he had a chance at a much higher paying job.

"Ma! Ma!" Connor called as he burst through the door to the shanty.

His mother was bent over a tub washing clothes on her scrub board. She looked up wiping the sweat off her forehead with her forearm. Her beautiful red hair was plastered to her face with sweat from her hard work. Little Bridget was playing with a ragged doll next to where her mother worked. Despite the surroundings her clothes and face were clean. His mother was adamant about staying clean. She had told Connor:

"We may not have much money but we will always present ourselves as who we are. We will not give in to our present circumstances. You will always wear a clean shirt and pants even if you have to wash them yourself before you leave this house."

She had been right, it was one of the reasons the station-agent had given him the job as a callboy. Now he was offering him a promotion. He had looked at Connor for a moment before he said.

"Boy, you show up every day clean as a whistle. That's what I need, a boy who can present himself well for this job."

The door slammed behind Connor and only the light through the one small window illuminated the shack. The shaft of light was filled with smoke and dirt from the rail yard making his mother's job of keeping the place clean even harder.

"Son what have I told you about slamming the door?"

"Sorry Ma. It's just that I got a little excited. I've been offered a promotion."

His mother turned toward him and put her

hands on her hips and said.

"Do tell."

His Ma did not like him working on the railroad. It was considered one of the most dangerous jobs anyone could have. Hardly a week went by that a man was not maimed or killed in the train yard not far from their home.

Brakemen were crushed between cars as they ran alongside the freight cars to slip a pin into the coupling. Others died when they fell off moving trains as they worked the brake wheels. Still, others were killed in train wrecks that happened too frequently. Railroading was still a new and growing industry and the mechanical systems had not kept up with the rapid growth and seemingly endless demand. Railroading was growing so fast his father had told him that he might just stay with the railroad instead of going west. All of that changed when he died.

"Ma. They want me to be a butcher boy on tonight's seven ten to Topeka."

His mother frowned.

"Butcher boy?"

"Yes, it's not like it sounds. It would be my job to bring drinks and sell snacks and books to the passengers. They tip the butcher boy. I would make double what I do as a call boy."

"I don't like it. I don't want you riding on those trains you know how I feel," his mother said with a frown.

"But Ma I wouldn't be doing anything dangerous. I wouldn't be a brakeman or fireman climbing around the train. My job would be inside with passengers, getting them water and such. Depending on the conductor I could sell snacks eventually. I get to keep all the tips in addition to the salary."

His mother just stared at him. She had been so

beautiful when his father was alive but the hard work and stress of raising two children by herself was beginning to show. He wanted to help more. Sure he was only twelve but he was big for his age and looked and acted older.

"What happened to the last boy?"

"He had no manners and was stealing from the old ladies. The conductor caught him and threw him off his train and told him to never come back."

"Your job would be to take care of the passengers and that's it?"

"Yes, Ma. I would be riding in those beautiful yellow cars with fancy seats. All I would be doing is bringing them water or a snack and do what the conductor wanted me too."

"Tonight?"

"Yes, Ma. It's just like when I was a callboy. They need somebody right now or they will find somebody else."

His mother said nothing as she thought about sending her son off to work on the railroad. Little Bridget looked up from where she was sitting on the floor and said.

"I like those yellow cars. Connor that would be fun to ride in them."

His mother smiled and said.

"I guess it would be all right since you will be safe in the car with passengers."

Connor did everything he could to keep from jumping with joy, as calmly as he could he said.

"Ma, the Station Master said the main reason he was hiring me is because I always presented myself well with clean clothes."

His mother smiled again.

"I told you one day all the work would be worth it."

"I'll need my best blue shirt, pants and my

bowtie."

Connor threw on his best clothes, plastered his hair down with water and shined his shoes. When he was ready he ran out the door headed for the roundhouse where the train would be put together.

Chapter 3

Connor left the shanty house at a dead run through the rail yard. The rail yard was loud, noisy and smoky as engines and cars were moved around. He loved it. Trains were leaving all the time. Some would head west with passengers and merchandise, while others would head east with cattle and other goods from the west. Switch engines moved back and forth taking freight cars or passenger cars to the right track to put together trains. It felt like Connor was at the center of the great movement to the west. He could almost feel America growing when he was at the rail yard.

He crossed track after track as he headed for the roundhouse where the seven fifteen to Topeka was being put together. The yard was busy as usual with passenger, freight cars and engines being moved around the yard as trains were disassembled and others were put together. Brakemen and yardmen jumped between and on top of the rail cars as they were connected to their trains.

The yard was filled with the sound and the clang of metal as cars were coupled. Engineers blew their steam whistles as trains left or entered the yards. Each engineer had his own whistle. If you knew their whistle you could tell if the engineer was leaving or coming home after a run. Connor was now a part of all of this. Before he had just found crewmembers when they were needed for a run, now, he was a crewmember.

He leaped over the iron rail of track after track as he headed across the yard. He was running to catch his train. The very thought made his stomach tighten with excitement. He was going to become a railroad man. His father would be proud he had become part of the railroad. Pa said it was the future of the United States. Now he would be a part of that future.

He flew over the tracks until he reached the far side of the yard. That's when Jake stepped out from behind a shed. Jake was one of the train boys. They were orphan boys who lived by their wits and hitching rides on the trains. Jake towered over Connor he was almost as tall as a man and just as strong. Some of the other boys said he carried a knife and knew how to use it.

Connor had avoided him as much as he could, but they had crossed paths a couple of times. Jake wanted money, and he had stopped Connor twice when he thought the station agent had just paid him. Both times he had no money, and Jake had just shoved him down and walked off.

"Where you headed boy all dressed up like you're going to church?" Jake asked.

"I got a job as a butcher boy and my train leaves soon."

"Which one?"

"The seven ten to Topeka."

Connor tried to run past him, but Jake stopped him with one big arm.

"They got a seven ten leaving tonight uh?" Jake said.

"Yeah and I gotta go, or I'll be late."

Connor tried to run around Jake, but he grabbed him. Connor tried to push his hands off of him, but he was too big and strong.

"Let me go, Jake. I ain't done nothing to you," Connor said.

"Yeah, but you're working the seven-ten to Topeka, and I need to get out of this town."

Connor looked up at Jake. No matter how big and tough he was Jake was not going to stop him from being on time for his new job. His mother and sister depended on him, and he was not going to let them down. Jake leaned down, so his face was close to Connor's and said.

"Listen, boy. The law is looking for me, and I need to get out of town before they catch up. So you're gonna help me jump that train."

Connor couldn't risk helping Jake. He could lose his job before he had even had a chance to prove himself. Suddenly he didn't care how big or tough Jake was, he was going to be on time no matter what it took.

"Darn if I will. You jump that train or not. I don't care. All I care about is being on time. Now let me go."

Connor kicked Jake in the shin as hard as he could.

"Ouch..."

Jake let Connor go and grabbed his leg with both hands. Connor took off running for the roundhouse where the engine would be. When he saw the engine standing on the roundhouse turntable, the sight stopped him dead in his tracks.

It had a polished black cab with gold leaf decorations. Every handrail, rod, and step gleamed in the sunlight. The big number forty-eight was painted on the side of the cab. It was Jack Killeen's engine he was considered the best engineer on the line. Connor was going to be part of one of the best crews.

He was standing there admiring the train when suddenly a huge hand grabbed him by the scuff of the neck.

Chapter 4

The hand lifted him off the ground as if he weighed nothing and set him down between two sets of tracks. He turned just in time to see a freight car roll over the spot where he had just been standing. The car was so close he could have reached out and touched its side. Fear flooded him as he realized he had almost been killed. If it hadn't been for the person who had grabbed him, the car would have crushed him.

The man standing next to him was huge with long muscular arms and a big mustache. A greasy engineer's cap was tilted on the back of his head. He wore a black thousand-mile shirt the way all the engineers did. It hid the dirt and grime that was part of their job. He looked down at Connor with hard blue eyes and said.

"Boy, never stand in the middle of a track in the yards. And before you cross always look both ways. Otherwise, you're gonna end up pushing up daisies."

"Yes, yes sir," Connor stammered.

"Now what are you doing out here in the middle of the yard all dressed up?" the man asked.

"I..I work on that train. Today's my first day as a butcher," Connor said pointing to old number 48.

The man spit before he said.

"Boy my name is Killeen and that there's my train. I'm the engineer so you're part of my crew and I don't aim to lose anyone. Now you run along and report to the Captain."

"Yes, sir."

Connor started to run across the tracks to the train but stopped himself and looked both ways before he did.

"Good boy. You might just live long enough to become an engineer someday if you step lively and pay attention."

Connor raced to the shop where engine Number 48 sat. He was careful each time he stepped over the rails as he searched for the conductor. The shop was a huge vast building with rolling doors. Clouds of dust and metal filing floated in the light from the windows. Men moved in and around the engines repairing and servicing them.

Connor realized just how loud the shop was as he got closer. Men shouted as they moved massive engine parts, steam hissed from the engines and the clanging of the mechanics' tools all combined into one overwhelming din. The floor was a maze of engine parts, tools, headlights, and brass fittings. It all added up to be a very overwhelming place. He stepped carefully into the dark interior of the shop. Looking for the Captain of his train.

He didn't want to be late for his first meeting with the conductor. He would be his boss and determine if he got the job and held it. The conductors were called Captains because they were responsible for keeping; the train on time, the passengers happy and making sure the luggage and freight all were on board. It was a big responsibility, and only the best worked their way up to being the conductor on a mainline passenger train. He found his conductor Shin McDougall standing with Jack Killian the engineer who had just saved his life. They had their pocket watches out and were comparing the time.

Killian had gotten there first because Connor had become lost in the huge shop. He even asked for directions. When he ran up to McDougall, he touched his cap and said.

"Connor Galway reporting for duty sir."

The man looked him over before he said.

"Bought time you got here boy. We about left you. This here is my engineer."

Connor touched his cap to Killian who smiled and said.

"We done met. We almost lost the boy in the yard. Nice to see you son."

Before Connor could ask how he had gotten here so fast, McDougall said.

"Times a wasting boy we got to take on water and wood."

The conductor and engineer walked over Number 48. It was the first time Connor had ever been this close to an engine before. He had seen them every day in the yard, coming and going, belching steam and smoke. While he had worked for the railroad for almost a year, he had never been this close to an engine. It was a sight to behold.

The metal giant towered over him gleaming in the late afternoon sun. It almost seemed alive as steam hissed out of valves releasing pressure, metal clanged as it heated and cooled. It was like some powerful mechanical beast anxious to get going, eager to move down the rails. Connor followed Killian and McDougall to the engine. They quickly stepped up into the cab while Connor stood there staring not knowing where he should be.

"Boy, you ride with me."

Connor turned to see a short, stocky man behind him.

"I'm the brakeman, O'Brian, son. Just do what I do."

O'Brian grabbed a handrail and swung up on the side step of the engine. Connor walked over to the engine reached up and grabbed the rail just as O'Brian had done. He could feel it vibrate as the engine idled waiting for the engineer to set it free.

It was alive, Connor thought. He swung up on the step alongside the brakeman. He felt like a real railroad man now that he was riding with his crew on a real engine. His chest filled with pride as Killian gave the 48 a whisper of steam and it slid out of the roundhouse and onto a track. For the first time in his life, he felt the wind in his face from the movement of a train. Connor watched as the ground sped past his feet as he stood on the side step. Connor had to fight the urge to yell, he was so excited but remained quiet. He wanted to look like he knew what he was doing. While the other men had done this for most of their lives, for Connor, it meant he was a railroad man.

Chapter 5

As the engine moved across the yards

Killeen, the engineer looked back at him and said.

"Come on up here boy. Ride in the cab with

me."

Connor scrambled across the car and up

into the cab. He could hardly believe that he was

actually standing next to one of the best

engineers on the line. Old number 48 moved quickly through the yard under Killeen's hand.

Connor's eyes followed Killeen as his hand moved with practiced ease over the controls of the engine. One day he could become an engineer like Killeen, Connor thought.

They switched tracks and headed for the woodpile. They would load the tender with wood the engine would need for the trip. Everyone jumped down off the engine and began to load the tender. McDougall had Connor stand on the platform of the engine while O'Brian handed wood from the pile to him. Connor loaded the firebox on the engine first then the tender with wood.

He and O'Brian became a good team. O'Brian was a young man not too many years older than Connor but be he had the look of a railroad man. Conductor McDougall stood to one side watching the time as they loaded the wood on board. When they had filled the firebox and tender McDougall said.

"Right on time boys. Mr. Killeen if you give her some steam we will pick up our train."

Killeen eased the throttle, and the train slid down the tracks to where the yellow passenger cars trimmed in black, a baggage car and a caboose waited for them. Killeen backed the engine onto the siding and slipped the coupling onto the waiting rail cars. O'Brian jumped between the cars and slipped in the pin into the coupling. He scrambled up the car to its roof where he would spend most of the trip and signaled all was ready.

Then without so much as a jerk, Killeen pulled the train out of the siding and headed for the station. Connor could hardly take his eyes off Killeen's hands as they moved with years of practice from the live steam injector to the throttle. His eyes always monitoring the pressure gauges as the engine built up steam. He glanced over at Connor and said.

"You always let her build her head at first. She needs to get the feel of the cars."

Connor was amazed that the engineer talked about the engine as if it was a living thing.

"Yeah, boy. You treat her right, and she'll take care of you. Now you better get back where you belong before McDougall decides to box your ears."

Killeen slowed the train as it approached the station. The platform was filled with people waiting for it. Carriages and hacks with their horses hitched to the rails were crowded around the station as baggage and passengers unloaded for the trip. Fashionable women with large hats, long skirts and parasols stood beside men in broad hats with large waxed mustaches.

Several small tables were set up on the station platform for the passengers. They sold everything a passenger might want. There was hot beefsteak, slices of cold roast antelope, cold chicken, ham and poached eggs and to drink there was cold sweet tea and coffee. Some sold postcards, salted nuts, magazines, newspapers and candy, almost anything a passenger could want. It had the look of a festival with all the comings and goings and people selling their wares.

Connor jumped off and ran back to the passenger cars. McDougall stepped from the train to the platform. He had put on all of the finery of his authority on the train. McDougall wore a top hat with a metal badge on the front that read conductor with a fine coat of broadcloth as nice as any passenger. He had put on yellow kid gloves with paper money between his fingers to give change to the passengers for their fares.

His lantern hung on the platform beside him. It was silver plated while the upper half of the glass was blue and the lower half clear. In one hand he held a gold plated ticket punch. Connor had never seen a conductor dressed as fancy as Mr. McDougall. The passengers began to board the train and as they did the greeted Mr. McDougall.

"Nice to see you again Captain," a traveling salesman said.

"Nice to see you too. Been a while since you made this run."

"Yes, yes it has. It's nice to see you. I know I'm on a well-run train."

"Thank you, sir," McDougall said as he punched his ticket.

Connor approached not sure what he should do. With a frown, McDougall motioned for him to stand beside him. Connor did with his hands behind this back. As the men and women boarded, Connor looked around the station. To his right behind the station, he saw two heads peek out from behind the wall one was Big Jake.

Jake and the other boys were different than Connor. They had to find a way to live on their own because none had families. Some had lost their parents to the fever that had killed his father. Other families were so poor that they had left to make it easier for them to take care of their brothers and sisters.

Connor had listened to them talk of all the places they had been and which line was easiest to hitch a ride on to avoid the railroad police. They lived by their wits and what they could steal, in a way they seemed adventurous to Connor. He couldn't say if he would not be the same if he didn't have a mother and little sister.

When Jake saw him notice them, they ducked back behind the station. That is when Connor knew what Jack was going to do. He was going to try and jump the train! Should he tell Mr. McDougall? Connor turned to tell Mr. McDougall about Jake when Mr. McDougall said.

"Boy go fill our water jug before we take the last of the passengers on board."

Connor touched his cap and said.

"Yes, sir."

Connor ran and grabbed the water jug out of the passenger car and filled it from the pump on the side of the station house. He never saw where Jake and his friend went. With his jug full, Connor stepped onto the rear platform of the passenger car.

It was the first time in his life he had stepped into a real railroad passenger car. It was a long car with an aisle down the middle and passenger seats on each side. It was the most elegant place he had ever seen.

The ceilings were linoleum, each bench was covered with blue velvet, polished brass oil lamps hung from the ceiling, and an ornate wood stove stood at the other end of the coach. The furnace had a silver handle and decorations. The woodwork was hand carved and highly polished. It looked like a rich man's room on wheels. Even the house he had lived in when his father was alive was not nearly as fancy as this coach.

"Boy step aside so our passengers can pass," McDougall snapped.

Connor stepped into the space between seats so a woman with her young daughter could pass. They both were dressed in fine linen with long skirts and hats that tilted forward. They carried a wicker hamper filled with food to eat during the trip. Connor caught a whiff of the food as they passed. As they brushed past him, the older woman gave him a sharp look, but the girl smiled at him. They moved down the aisle until they found a seat in the middle of the car. They sat down and put their wicker basket on the floor at their feet.

Next, came a tall, lean man with the look of someone who had worked hard all his life. He had a long deep scar down the side of his face that disappeared into his large dropping mustache. As he moved past Connor, he saw under his long coat a large colt revolver tucked into his belt on one side. On the other side, he wore a big bowie knife in a scabbard. He carried a big bag made of old carpet that looked as if it had been used for a long time before it became his traveling bag.

When he moved past Connor, the bag brushed against him, it almost knocked him down since it was so heavy. Connor drew back from the man; he had an air of danger about him. The man found a seat on the left side of the car. He easily swung the heavy bag into the overhead baggage shelf and sat by the window. Other passengers looking for seats gave him a wide berth and sat several seats away from him.

"Captain," Connor said quietly to the conductor. "That man has a revolver and knife. Could he be an outlaw?"

The conductor turned and looked the man over closely.

"No, boy. It may be that he lives in rough places, but he's no outlaw."

"How do you know Captain?"

"No, outlaw would pay for a seat or have any luggage. They find other ways to get aboard."

Connor looked back at the man. He was staring out the window at the station like any other passenger, but he still made Connor feel uncomfortable. The rest of the passengers boarded and found their seats. When the last of those standing on the platform had boarded Mr. McDougall looked up and down the platform then said.

"All aboard."

When no more passengers came running, he swung his lantern back and forth, and the train slid smoothly down the tracks. Connor was standing behind McDougall as they pulled out of the station. He thought his heart would jump out of his chest; he was so excited. The train slowly pulled into the yard, and the switchmen set it on the right track, as the train left the yard gathering speed. For the first time in his life, Connor felt the pure excitement of leaving the only place he had ever known on a train.

Chapter 6

They had been on the road for over a couple of hours. Connor was refilling his pitcher of water from the jug on the platform when he thought he heard a voice. He looked around and saw nothing. All he heard was the roar of the engine and the clickity-clack of the wheels on the rails.

"Hey, you!"

This time there was no doubt he had heard someone. Connor again looked out in the dark night but saw no one.

"Down here, you idiot."

Connor looked down between the two rail cars and saw Jake the yard boy hanging beneath the platform of the baggage car.

"What the..."

"You've got a hot box on the rear baggage car."

"What?"

"A hot box. It's burning good."

Connor put his pitcher down and grabbed the railing on the car's platform. He leaned out into the wind and looked toward the rear of the train. Sure enough, flames were blowing out of the rear wheels of the baggage car. It was a hot box for sure.

A hot box was when the packing of cotton and oily rags around the axle caught fire. If it wasn't found in time, it could catch the whole car on fire or even cause a wreck. Connor turned to run inside and tell McDougall as he did he glanced down and Jake was gone. He ran down the aisle found McDougall talking to one of the passengers.

"Yes, ma'am. We are on schedule."

Connor pulled on his sleeve. He didn't want to scare the passengers, so he said.

"Sir, can I have a word."

McDougall shook him off with a scowl.

"The boy doesn't know better than to interrupt when his elders are speaking."

Connor pulled on his sleeve again and when McDougall saw the look of fear on his face he said.

"Excuse me, ma'am, this might be important."

McDougall led Connor down the aisle to a place in the car where there were no passengers and said.

"Boy this had better be good."

"We got a hot box on the rear of the baggage car."

McDougall shoved his way past Connor and rushed out onto the platform. He leaned out into the wind and saw the flames spewing out of the rear wheel box. He grabbed his lantern and began to wave it so the engineer would take notice.

To Connor, it seemed to take forever before the train started to slow down. It finally came to a stop and Connor followed McDougall as he jumped down to the ground. Johnson, the fireman, came running up followed by Killeen, the engineer.

"Hop to it boys. Let's get this out," Killeen ordered. "You help them boy."

"I don't know what to do," Connor said.

"Don't worry they'll tell you.

"Boy grab that bucket from the railing there and fill it with some water," Killeen said.

Connor grabbed the bucket from his hook on the railing on the car's platform. He filled it with water from his jug. Then struggled down the steps to the ground.

"Don't be shy throw her on there," Johnson said.

Connor swung the bucket throwing the water on the fire showing from the box. With a loud hissing noise, the fire went out.

"Good going we got it from here."

Johnson and O'Brian immediately went to work. They grabbed wrenches from the toolbox in the baggage car and began to turn the lugs on the red-hot box. As they worked, Connor looked around for Jake. He was nowhere to be found. He saw the rods under the car that gave the car stability had a small space between the bar and the bottom of the car. It must be where Jake had been riding. Connor had heard of hobos riding under there but he never thought someone his own age could do it.

"Son you saved us from a real problem. How did you spot it?" Killeen the engineer asked.

"Oh, uh. Something caught my eye when I was filling my pitcher."

"Good thing it did or we'd all be in trouble."

Johnson and O'Brian had the cover off and had Connor put another bucket of water on the box to cool it down before they repacked it. Connor was amazed at how quickly they had the box put back together and they were ready to roll. The crew scrambled back on board and McDougall stood on the car's platform and swung his lantern signaling the engineer they were ready.

Killeen blew the steam whistle twice and the train began to move again.

Chapter 7

    The train had been rolling along for an hour and had just made it over a very large steep hill. Connor could feel it start down the other side. He had just made a walk through the cars offering the passengers water when he felt the grade getting much steeper. He had to brace himself against one of the seats to stand it was so steep.

He stood there waiting for the grade to flatten out when he heard the engineer pull the steam whistle.

Whoooo. Whoooo. Whooo. Whooo.

The train was picking up speed. The steam whistle of the engine sounded again.

Whoooo.Whoooo. Whoooo. Whoooo.

Four long whistles. Then they started again.

Whoooo.Whoooo. Whoooo. Whoooo.

What was going on? Connor had never heard the engineer blow his whistle like that before. McDougall suddenly burst into the car from the rear of the train. He had been checking tickets. He rushed up to Connor and said in a whisper as he pulled him by the arm out onto the car's platform.

"Boy the train is broke in two. The brakeman is with the engineer. You and I will have to slow the cars before we crash into the front of the train. Now up the ladder, you go. Watch what I do and brake when I do. No more or we will wreck. You go up top here, and I'll go forward."

The conductor turned and ran forward through the car. Connor's heart was about to pound out of his chest. A train broke in two was one of the worst things that could happen. It meant that the rear of the train had come uncoupled from the engine and the front of the train. The back would pick up speed until it rammed into the engine and the rest of the train. The only way to avoid it was for the brakeman to slow the rear of the train before the crash. The brakeman was forward with the engineer according to the Captain, now it was up to him and the conductor to slow the train.

He climbed on the railing and reached out to grab the ladder that led to the roof of the car.

The wind was howling as he climbed the ladder. The rear of the train continued to pick up speed going faster and faster down the hill. Connor reached the top of the car. He glanced down and saw how far down the ground appeared. The wind was so strong it almost tore his cap from his head.

He reached out and grabbed the brake wheel so he could pull himself up onto the roof of the swaying car. If he fell, well Connor didn't want to think about that. He carefully gripped the iron wheel as he climbed up onto the roof of the swaying rail car. He stood holding onto the brake wheel with both hands the wind howling past him. When he was steady, he looked toward the engine. Black smoke was pouring out of the stack as the engineer put the throttle to the engine. Their only chance was for the engineer to pick up enough speed to outrun the rear of the train until the back of the train could be slowed.

He looked forward in the dark to see if the conductor had reached the roof of the car in front of him. At first, he saw nothing then he finally made out the outline of McDougall in the darkness. He was on top of the car at the brake wheel. He was looking back waiting for Connor to get in place. When he saw Connor was ready, he yelled.

"Turn her for all she's worth boy," he screamed over the howling wind.

McDougall was turning his brake wheel. So Connor grabbed the big iron brake wheel and tried to turn it. It barely budged. The cars were going faster and faster the brakes weren't slowing them.

"Put your back into it boy!" McDougall screamed. "Use the club!"

There was a club that was stuck through the wheel, it looked like a baseball bat. Connor grabbed it and stuck it through the rungs of the wheel. It gave it more leverage to turn the wheel. Connor bent his legs, used both hands, leaned back and pulled with all his might. The wheel began to turn. Sparks flew from the wheels on the rails as they began to slow. Connor continued to pull for all he was worth. McDougall looked back and saw him starting to turn the wheel.

"That's it boy pull!" he yelled.

Connor did it again, and the wheel turned more this time, and he could feel the train beginning to slow. Sparks flew even higher as the brake slowed the wheel. The wind howled in his ears, and the engine roared even louder.

Killeen was leaning on the throttle to try and outrun the rear cars. The smoke out of the engines stack was filled with sparks as the fireman fed the engine's firebox all the wood he could. Connor pulled on the brake wheel again when McDougall did. More sparks few but now he could really feel the cars slowing.

The distance between the broke away cars, and the engine began to increase. Connor pulled again, and the rear section of the train slowed even more as the engine raced down the steep grade. Connor continued to twist the brake whenever McDougall did until the back part of the train slowly came to a stop at the bottom of the grade.

When Killeen saw the breakaway come to a stop, he slowed the engine to a halt. He reversed it and slowly backed towards the wayward rear of the train. O'Brian jumped off the engine's tender and was ready to re-couple the train when they slowly came together. He slipped a pin into the coupling, and the train was no longer broken in two. He signaled Killeen, and with a bit of a jerk the train moved forward.

Connor climbed down the ladder and jumped between the two cars onto the rear platform of the passenger car. The tall man with the scar on his face suddenly loomed out of the darkness startling Connor. He looked down at him and said.

"Nice job boy."

Connor was so startled by his kind words; he almost didn't touch his cap before he said.

"Thank you, sir."

The man just turned and returned to his seat without another word. Connor would have never expected a kind word from a man like that. Maybe he had been wrong about him, but he sure did look dangerous.

Chapter 8

McDougall and the brakeman O'Brian came out on the platform.

"Well done boy," O'Brian said patting him on the back.

McDougall looked at O'Brian a furious look on his face and said.

"It was your job, O'Brian. The boy should never have had to do it. Where were you?"

"The fireman had asked for some help with firing the box for the grade. I was helping him."

"Not on my train. You have a job now stick to it, or this will be the last run you'll make on my train. I'll speak to the fireman myself when I get the chance. Do you understand?"

O'Brian looked angry but only touched his cap and said.

"Aye Captain."

He turned, and with well-practiced agility, he climbed to the roof of the car to his normal position. McDougall looked down at Connor and said.

"Son you might just make a real railroad man someday if you keep working like that. Braking a broke in two train will make a man of you. Your father would have been proud."

Pride swelled in Connor's chest with the compliment.

"Thank you, Captain."

"Now get back to work. If someone asks just say, there was a minor problem with the brakes. We don't want to scare the passengers."

"Yes, sir."

Connor entered the car and grabbed his tray. He filled the glasses with water and went down the aisle offering the passengers a drink. The woman with a massive hat with an ostrich feather took one of the glasses and said.

"What was all that commotion boy? And why did we stop?"

Before Connor could answer, McDougall had come up behind him and said.

"Ma'am. Nothing to worry your head about. Just the normal grade on this run and there were some cows on the tracks we had to stop for."

"Will we be on time? I did not buy a ticket on this line to be late."

McDougall pulled his railroad pocket watch out of his vest and checked the time. The man with the scar met Connor's eyes and gave him a small smile and a nod. He knew what had happened but wasn't going to say anything that might scare the other passengers.

"Yes, ma'am. This train will be on time. The engineer will increase the speed just enough to make up what we lost back there. My train always runs on time."

Connor glanced back at the conductor who winked at him and gently touched his back urging him on down the car so he could serve the other passengers. Connor went down the aisle offering water.

The Captain had said he might make a real railroad man someday. He was just a boy and now a conductor was telling him he had done a good job. The man with the scar had even noticed. For the first time in his life, Connor felt as if he had grown up.

He had proven himself in a dangerous situation. He now knew he could do the job of a man if he put his mind and back to it. This was a very fine day. He knew that he had earned a position on this train. A job meant he could really help his mother and sister. He could make enough money now to help with buying food and rent.

Connor refilled his jug and cleaned some glasses before he went back down the aisle. The train sped down the track into the night. He looked outside and thought it was a beautiful night with the stars bright and the wind whipping past. It was a railroad man's night.

Chapter 9

The passengers had settled into their seats, some were even sleeping. Suddenly a tremendous noise of metal being torn apart filled the car.

Screech!

Then the car began to bounce violently on the railroad ties not on the tracks. It was all

Connor could do not to be thrown to the floor. He held onto a back seat with all his strength. An oil lantern from the ceiling fell to the floor. A woman's hat box flew across the car. Then there was a jolt as if the car had hit something.

Bang!

The car tipped over to the right throwing Connor into the air.

Crash!

Wood splinters filled the car. Luggage from the racks over the seats began to fall. This all combined into one terrifying sound. Connor had never heard a sound like that before.

Rumble..crunch..bang!

"Oh, no!" a woman screamed.

Connor landed between two seats. The car had landed completely on it's right side. He looked up to see the seats that had been on the left side of the car now were above him. There was another tremendous jolt. The front of the car crashed inward.

Wood splinters a foot long flew through the car above Connor's head. The car began to slow down then stopped. All of a sudden there were no more sounds. Everything was very quiet. It was a strange silence after all of the noise.

Connor started to stand up when he heard a groaning noise above him. He looked up to see one of the seats break from the bolts holding it to the floor. It came crashing toward Connor. Connor curled into a tight ball hoping that the bench seat would not hit him. It crashed on top of him missing most of him but pinning one of his legs underneath it. The weight of the seat on Connor's leg hurt. He groaned in pain. Then he heard another sound.

Screech!

More metal being torn apart. Connor looked up to see the pot-bellied stove slowly swing away from its base and fall. It crashed into the seats just behind Connor.

The stove's door flew open, and coals and fire were thrown all over the upholstered seats. They immediately burst into flame. The seats just behind Connor began to burn. The fire would soon reach the seats Connor was crouched under.

Desperately he tried to pull his leg out from under the seat but he couldn't it was too heavy. He could feel the heat of the fire through his shoes as it grew.

"Oh, please help me!" a woman screamed.

Connor wanted to help. He was a railroad man now, and you had to help the passengers, but he was trapped. He pushed against the seat with all his might, but it wouldn't move. He could see flames above the seat now the fire was growing quickly. He had to do something.

"Here boy."

Connor looked up and saw the man with the long scar standing over him. His head was bleeding, but it didn't seem to faze him.

"I'm trapped. I can't get my leg out."

The man grabbed a carpetbag and threw it aside to make more room. Then with one mighty shove, he moved another seat that had fallen from the pile pinning Connor's leg.

"Now boy," he said.

Connor pushed against the seat on his leg and tried to pull his leg out.

"It won't move!"

The man moved closer to the fire and gripped the seat on top of Connor's leg.

"Boy when I count to three, you push, and I will pull."

"Ok."

"One."

The flames were getting bigger.

"Two."

Connor could feel the heat on his foot now. It was almost too much to stand.

"Three!"

Connor shoved the seat with his hands and his one free foot. The man with the scar groaned as he strained to pull the bench up just a few inches. The seat began to move inch by inch until Connor was able to pull his leg out from under it.

With a sigh the man let the seat fall back. Connor scrambled to his feet. The flames were now almost as tall as he was. He looked at the man with the scar in the firelight and said.

"We have to put out the fire!"

Chapter 10

"How do we do that boy?" the man asked.

Connor knew where the bucket he had used on the hot box had been stored. He could only hope he could find it in time.

"The car's bucket. It's there on the other side of the fire."

"You can't..."

Connor as quick as a squirrel climbed through a tree he scrambled through the wreckage. As he neared the fire, he held his breath and jumped over the flaming wreckage. He landed on his feet clear of the flames and made his way to the rear door.

When he looked back he realized that a man could never have made it past the fire he was too big. The wreckage had only left an opening large enough for Connor to squeeze through. The man with the scar was helping the other passengers, but unless Connor could put out the fire, it wouldn't matter they all would burn up.

The platform was a jumble of bent and torn metal. The hook where the bucket was kept was gone. So were the bucket and jug where Connor got his water for the passengers. With the light from the growing fire, Connor frantically looked around for it, but he didn't see it anywhere.

"What are you looking for?" a voice from the darkness said.

Connor looked and saw Jake standing next to the wrecked cars.

"You're alive?"

"Not by much. What are you looking for?"

"A bucket I've got to put the fire out."

Jake immediately began to look around the wreck for a bucket. Connor spotted it behind Jake.

"Jake behind you."

Jake grabbed the bucket and tossed it to Connor. Connor had thought of his big jug as the source of water, but when he turned, he found it crushed under the metal railing of the car.

"I need water. The jugs broke," Connor yelled to Jake.

Jake looked around and then shouted.

"There's a ditch with water in it. Toss me the bucket."

Connor tossed him the bucket and Jake scooped it full of water then struggled back up the bank to the crash and handed it to Connor. Connor grabbed the handle. The bucket was heavy filled with water, he couldn't lift it with just one hand. He had to use two hands to pull it up and over the wreckage. He turned and stumbled and climbed back into the car trying to spill as little of the water as he could. The fire was licking at the seats at the top of the car now. When the tall man with the scar saw him, he shouted.

"Hurry up boy, we don't have much longer."

Connor braced his back against what used to be the door to the platform and tossed the bucket of water onto the fire. The flames darkened down, and the metal stove hissed as the cold water met the hot metal.

"Good job, but she needs more boy."

Connor climbed back out onto the wreckage of the platform and looked for Jake. He was waiting.

"More. We need more."

Connor tossed him the bucket and Jake ran down the bank to the ditch and filled the bucket again. He scrambled up the bank and handed Connor the bucket. It was then that Connor realized that Jake was acting as part of the crew and not just some rail boy looking to get a free ride. He was helping because help was needed and it didn't matter who you were, it only mattered if you were willing to help.

His father had told him to judge a man by how he acts when things get tough. His father had been in the war and said that a man was judged by how he performed in battle. Not by who his family was or how much money he had, it only mattered if he would stand beside you in a fight. This was like a battle and Jake was proving himself a man who could be counted on in time of trouble.

Jake came back with another bucket of water and handed it up to Connor. He climbed over the platform and back into the wreckage of the car. He was able to get close to the fire now. The main body of the fire was out, but a few stubborn flames were still trying to spread. Connor carefully poured the water onto the flames, and they went out with a hiss. The inside of the stove was still red hot with coals from the fire. The water wasn't reaching them; he would have to put them out too.

One more time Connor climbed back over the wreckage. He was exhausted, but he knew he couldn't stop; people's lives depended on him. He made it to the platform a third time, and Jake was waiting for him.

"One more Jake."

He tossed the bucket down to him, and one more time Jake scrambled down the embankment to the ditch and brought back a bucket of water. The bucket seemed heavier than ever, and it took all of Connor's strength to climb back through the wreckage with the heavy water bucket.

When he entered the car, Connor moved carefully until he was as close to the stove as he dared and then slowly poured the water into the open door of the stove. The glowing coals crackled and hissed as they turned black. The fire was out. Connor leaned back against the wreckage breathing heavily, exhausted.

"I need your help boy."

Connor turned to see the man with the scar working to free another passenger. New found energy surged through Connor, and he climbed over a seat and moved toward the man.

Chapter 11

Connor climbed over the jumble of seats, luggage and large pieces of wood crushed by the wreck towards the man with the scar. He was bent over a pair of seats that had been smashed together by the wreck. He was pulling at something Connor couldn't see. Connor climbed over the last bench seat and saw the woman who had worn the hat with the ostrich feather lying with part of the car's wall across her legs.

"Boy, we need to get her free. Grab that seat and see if you can move it. I can't get over there."

Connor scrambled down to the seat that was holding the wood across the legs of the woman. He had to lift it off of her legs somehow. He already knew how heavy the seats were and how hard they were to move. How was he going to do it?

Suddenly he remembered something his father had shown him about moving cumbersome boxes. He squeezed into the space between the seat and the wall of the car; he was just large enough to fit. He turned and put his back to the bench and squatted down on his heels.

"Ok, I'm ready."

"Ok, boy on three again. Heave with all your might."

Connor grabbed the bottom of the seat with both hands and got a good grip.

"One, two, three."

Connor pushed his legs with all his strength. The seat moved upward not much, but it moved. He kept pushing with his legs, harder and harder, the seat slowly began to move higher and higher. Connor heard the sound of the man and the woman scrambling behind him. He couldn't see what they were doing so he kept pushing, his arms and legs shaking with the effort. When he didn't think he could last another second, he heard the man say.

"Ok, boy. You can ease her down. She's free."

With a sigh of relief, Connor eased the seat back down. Then he stood and turned to face them a huge smile on his face. The man towered over the woman who was standing next to him in the wreckage.

"Good job again boy."

"Yes, son. Thank you," the woman said.

"My name is Connor."

Connor was getting tired of being called boy after he had been acting like a real railroad man this whole trip.

"Right you are Connor. Just call me Hermann. And this is Mrs. O'Toole."

"Hermann, have you seen the Captain?" Connor asked.

Connor just realized he had not seen the conductor.

"Last I saw him he was going forward to the baggage car. We need to get Mrs. O'Toole out of here. You're a monkey moving over this wreak. Can you find us a way out?"

"Yes, sir."

Connor scrambled over the wreckage worked his way towards what was left of the car looking for some way out of the debris. He had climbed over several seats when he saw the legs of the salesman with the bowler hat sticking out from under part of the car that had caved in on him. He started to move to help him when he heard Hermann say.

"He's gone, boy. I've already checked him. You find us a way out of here."

Connor didn't look any closer at the salesman, he concentrated on finding a way out. As he moved toward the front of the car, he realized that it had been more badly damaged in the crash than the rear where they had been. The wall on the right side had been crushed inward. The car was lying on its side, so one side of the car was blocked entirely. He had to find a way out of the wreckage at the front of the car. None of the passengers would be able to climb out the back the way he had. He had to find another way.

He ducked under some wreckage and squirmed his way through a small opening. It was like he was entering a cave. It was pitch black there was not even a hint of light. He took a moment to calm himself. People depended on him he couldn't let them down. He had to lie on his stomach to move through the wreckage. Ahead of him should be the door leading forward to the platform but he couldn't find a way out.

He felt around with his hands trying to figure out what was blocking him. Then he felt a metal rail and a carpetbag. Then his hand touched the rectangular shape of a suitcase. It was the luggage rack from above the seats it had been thrown forward and was blocking his way.

He started to push and pull on the carpetbag when he heard a voice from outside of the car.

"You in there are you all right?"

Connor knew that voice.

"Jake is that you?"

"Yeah, I got worried when you didn't come back out."

"We got people trapped in here. Can we get out this way?"

"Yeah, the whole side of the car is gone. It's only that luggage rack and all the luggage blocking from the looks of it."

"Great start pulling stuff on your side and I'll push."

Connor saw a carpetbag move so he pushed as hard as he could. Once again it was hard to move but he kept pushing and it slowly came free. Suddenly with a scraping sound, the carpetbag disappeared. Connor could see out into the night.

There standing in the light created by the fires in the other cars he saw Jake. In the orange light, he looked like a real railroad man. He grabbed the next bag, and they both started pushing and pulling. They almost had it out when Jake put his foot against the side of the train and pulled groaning with the effort. It popped free. When it did the wreckage above Connor's head groaned and lurched downward. He was going to be crushed!

"Connor!" Jake yelled.

Connor covered his head and waited for the weight of the train car to come crashing down on him.

Chapter 12

A wooden ceiling beam of the car came down with a groan and actually struck Connor lightly on the head before it bounced back up.

"That was close!" Jake yelled.

"You're telling me," Connor said trying to sound brave with his heart racing with fear. He had almost screamed when he felt the beam touch him. It took him a moment before he could gather himself to start to work again. He began pushing on the next piece of luggage when he said.

"You see any of the train crew?"

"Not yet. She's on her side from the engine to caboose. Engine still letting off steam and the first baggage car is burning a bit."

"What about other passengers?"

"A few are standing around out here, but we're going to need help to get the rest out."

"Let's get this done first," Connor said.

Working together the two were able to widen the hole enough for Connor to crawl out. What he saw stunned him. The whole train was lying on its side just like Jake said. The wood from the tender had spilled out in a big mound. The baggage car just behind the tender and in front of the passenger car was beginning to burn. He could see flames coming out of the sliding door.

Looking towards the rear of the train the other cars were also on their sides, just as Jake had said. It was a terrible sight seeing the fine train twisted and broken. He could see a couple of figures moving about in the darkness, but there was no real organized effort to help the others. Where were the Captain and the Engineer? They should be taking charge of things, all Connor saw was the wreckage and a few passengers in the firelight.

"Connor where are you boy?" Hermann from inside the car yelled.

Then Connor realized that Hermann, and the other passengers were waiting for him to find a way out.

"I made it out I need to find a bigger way for you," Connor yelled. "No adult could get through the way I did."

"Hurry up boy. We don't have long before something else goes wrong."

Connor couldn't worry about the rest of the crew it was up to him help the trapped passengers. He ran down the length of the car looking for the passenger to escape. The platforms at each end had been crushed so no adult could make their way through. What was he going to do? Then he saw a ladder that was usually attached to the platform, so the brakeman could climb up to the roof. It had been torn off and was lying on the ground, it looked just like a regular ladder instead of part of the car. That's when Connor realized what he could do.

"Jake help me."

Jake came running.

"What?"

"We can use this like a regular ladder, and I can get on top of the car. We're going to have to get them out that way."

"Okay

They each grabbed an end and tried to lift it. It was solid iron and heavier than any wooden ladder. It barely moved. Connor and Jake looked at one another.

"What are we going to do? This thing weighs a ton," Jake said.

Connor thought for a moment then said.

"Look we'll both lift one end and push it up against the car. Then we can climb right up."

Jake hesitated then said.

"You know I think that will work."

Connor ran down to Jake's end and grabbed the ladder, both strained to lift the iron ladder. With a lot of pulling then pushing they were able to raise the ladder up against the car. They steadied it to make sure it was safe to climb. Connor put his foot on the first rung to test it. It was solid so he scrambled up and onto the top of the car. Carefully walking on what used to be the side of the car he went to one of the windows. He could looked down and saw Hermann moving around inside below him.

"Hermann up here."

Hermann looked up and saw him in the window.

"Good boy but we're going to need a ladder to get out of here."

Connor looked over the side of the car and yelled at Jake.

"Are there any more ladders we could use to get everybody out?"

"I'll check."

Jake ran off into the night, Connor searched the side of the car to see if he could find anything else he could use as a ladder. Nothing. Then he ran back to the rear of the car. Jake came running up from the rear of the train.

"I've been up and down the train nothing. I can't find anything," Jake yelled.

Connor stood there on top of the train with people trapped just below him, and he couldn't get them out. There had to be a way.

"Hermann can you pile some luggage or something high enough so people could climb out."

Hermann smiled up at him and said.

"There you go thinking again boy."

Connor watched, and Hermann with the help of a couple of passengers piled some luggage up until they had enough for someone to climb the top of the car.

"You ready boy."

"Yeah send them up."

The first to climb up the pile of baggage and wreckage was the woman who had worn the big hat with the ostrich plume. Now her hat was gone, and her hair hung down her back. She carefully climbed up the makeshift pile and was soon standing next to Connor.

"Nice going son. Now what?"

"Over there is a ladder ma'am. Jake will help you down."

Carefully she found her way to the edge of the car and climbed down the ladder with Jake's help. It wasn't long before Connor, Hermann and the others were standing on the ground. Several of the passengers had patted Connor on the back when the Captain came running up. His head was bleeding, and one arm was tucked into this coat to give it support.

"I need every hand. The engineer is trapped, and the engine is still building steam."

"Where O'Brian sir?" Connor asked.

"He's gone son. Now we need to get to the engine."

Connor, Jake, and Hermann turned and followed the conductor into the night to the front of the train. As Connor ran he thought of O'Brian and how close they all had come to being killed.

Chapter 13

Connor ran behind the Conductor towards the steam engine. It was lying on its side. It was terrible to see such a fine, powerful engine lying all busted up like some wounded animal. Steam still hissed out of cracks and breaks in piping along its side. As they neared the wreckage, Connor and the others had to crawl over a mound of wood that had spilled out of the tender when the train had overturned. Connor and Jake were the first to make it over the mound of wood and get to the cab of the engine.

When Connor saw the wreckage all he could think of, was how beautiful and polished it had all been just hours ago. Now everything was bent or broken and covered with dirt and grime. That's when Connor heard a moan. Connor peered into the cab, but it was too dark to see anything.

"Mr. Killeen can you hear me," Connor yelled.

"Yes, yes. Who's that?"

"It's the butcher boy, sir. Connor."

"Glad to hear you boy."

"Are you trapped?"

"Yes, boy and Johnson the fireman is in even worse shape. I can't see him, but I can hear him."

Jake had climbed on top of the cab and was lying flat peering into the wreckage through the engine's cab window. He could just see Killeen, the engineer in the light from the firebox. He was lying on his back with one leg tangled in the throttle rod.

"They're pinned in there good Connor. Real good," Jake said.

Jake had climbed up onto the cab and lying beside him. He slowly shook his head. Before Connor could say anything, Killeen said from the wreckage.

"He's right boy. We're goners. Get away before the boiler blows. Save the passengers."

McDougall, the conductor, had just made his way over the wood spilled from the tender with Hermann by his side. He stood on the ground beside the engine one arm stuck in his coat for support. He could not climb up the wreckage to help.

"No, we won't Killeen. The passengers are safe. We're going to get you out of there," McDougall said. "We leave no man behind."

"Connor you're going to have to crawl in there. You're the smallest. I can't make it." Jake said.

"Right," Connor said.

He stared down into the darkness to find a place he could stand. He saw a part of the wreckage that would support him then get closer to Killeen. He slowly lowered himself down through the engineer's window. The inside of the cab was a tangle of broken wheels, pipes and gauges.

To his left were what remained of the instruments of the train. The steam pressure gauge, heating gauge, and water gauge were all broken. The door to the firebox was open, and the fire in the box illuminated the wreckage of the cab. Killeen was below him lying on his back. One leg was up in the air with the long regulator handle bent trapping the leg.

"Good to see you boy," Killeen said. "It's Johnson. I'm worried about."

"Where is he, Mr. Killeen?"

"He's under me and some wood from the tender."

"Are you hurt?"

"Yes, I think my leg's broke, and Johnson doesn't answer. He just groans when I try to talk to him."

Connor crawled closer until he could get a good look at the handle that was trapping

Killeen's leg. It was a long and round as three fingers on a man's hand. He put his hand on the handle and ran it up to where it connected to the boiler. When he tried to move it he realized it had been twisted by the wreck. The regulator handle controlled the amount of steam that went to the engine. Now it was a twisted mess trapping Killeen's leg.

"What have you got?" Jake yelled down from above. "The Captain wants to know."

"Killeen's trapped and Johnson's trapped under him."

"How bad are they hurt?"

"Killeen says his leg is broke. Don't know but Johnson only groans when Killeen talks to him."

Suddenly a value on the boiler in front of the cab burst and steam hissed out.

"The boilers still got a head of steam. Unless we can release it, she'll blow. Boy, you and your friend need to leave and get everybody away before she explodes," Killeen said.

Before Connor could say a word, the steam hissed even louder.

"Get out boy she's gonna blow!" Killeen shouted over the roar of the steam.

Connor turned and started to climb out.

"Give me your hand I'll pull you up!" Jake yelled.

Connor looked up to see Jake still in the cab's window waiting for him. He had never left even though the boiler was about to blow. Connor reached up and took Jake's hand as he started to climb out.

Chapter 14

Connor was almost at the window that led out of the cab, when it struck him. Railroad men don't leave their crews behind.

"Jake I can't leave them."

Jake looked at him, his face serious. He simply nodded and let go of Connor's hand. He began to climb back down into the cab.

"What are you doing boy? I told you to leave."

"A railroad man does not leave a crew member behind."

Killeen smiled and said.

"All right boy. But you're going to have to move fast. The steam is building. I don't know how much time we have. We're going to have to release the steam."

The boiler began to make a loud noise.

Creakkkkk!

"I don't know what to do. I have to get you free."

"Boy, we don't have time. I'll have to talk you through it."

Connor looked down at Killeen then up at Jake who was peering through the window. He was the only one who could do it. He had to do it.

"Ok. Tell me what to do."

Killeen shifted his position as much as he could so he could see the engine controls above him. He pointed to the open firebox door.

"Ok, boy here's what's happening. The firebox is still going. It's heating the boiler only the boiler has dumped most of its water. Eventually, the metal of the boiler will weaken from the heat, and the steam and rupture. She'll blow us all to kingdom come."

Connor looked at the wreckage of the cab of the engine with a knot of fear in his stomach. He was standing next to a bomb.

"What do I do?"

"You've got to climb up and find the steam safety valve."

"Where is it?"

"Somewhere above us in that jumble of wheels and pipes."

Connor looked up, and he couldn't tell what one thing did. It was all twisted into an unrecognizable mess. How could he ever find the safety valve in that mess?

"I can't make anything out."

"Ok, boy. Now I want you to put your foot on this rod, so you see higher."

When Connor stepped on the rod, Killeen groaned. He was hurting Killeen when he put his weight on the rod. Connor went to climb down when Killeen said.

"No, boy. It's all right; it's the only way."

Connor carefully put all his weight on the rod, and he was just high enough to see a row of wheels, with a second set behind the first set of controls. Suddenly there was a deafening metallic sound.

Crack!

The boiler sounded as if it were breaking.

"We gotta move fast boy that was the boiler beginning to give way."

"What do I do? It's a mess up here."

"Now listen to me. Behind the first row of the wheels there are two others. Can you see them?"

Crack!

The sound was even louder; the boiler sounded like it was about to explode. Connor couldn't see the other handles in the dark. He reached out with his hand to see if he could touch them. He was just able to feel two wheels.

"I can feel them."

"Good boy. Now it will be the one on your right. That is the safety valve. It will dump all of the steam pressure out of the boiler."

Moan.

Crack.

The boiler sounded like some kind of wounded animal. It couldn't last much longer. Connor almost gave up when he found the wheel to the right.

"Got it."

"Now turn it to the left. Quickly, boy, we don't have much time."

Connor's hand could barely reach the handle. He tried to turn it, but nothing happened. It wouldn't move.

"It won't move."

"Boy it's a hard one, but she will turn. Put your back into it."

Moan. Creak. Snap. Hiss.

Connor's almost ducked, the noise was so loud it sounded as if the boiler was finally going to explode. Steam suddenly began to vent out of the pan. It touched his hand and burned him. Then it stopped as quickly as it had started.

Connor had held on to the safety value wheel despite the pain in his hand where the steam had burned it.

Feeling the pain, the steam caused made Connor realize just how much danger they were in. Fear surged through him. He wanted to run away, but he gritted his teeth and held onto the wheel. The sudden fear gave him more strength than he knew he had. With all his might he was able to turn the wheel. Just a little at first then more and more.

Hisssss.

The steam was beginning to be released. He could hear the steam being discharged from a spigot outside of the cab. The hissing got louder and louder; the more he turned the valve.

"That's it, boy. You've got her now."

Connor kept turning the wheel until the hiss turned into a roar as the steam was released from the boiler.

"You did it, boy. You did it," Killeen yelled smiling from ear to ear.

"You did it Connor," Jake said.

Connor looked up to see Jake through the cab window. He had never left them. The roar continued for a while. Then it slowly got quieter as the last of the steam was released.

"You know boy standing on that rod sure does hurt my leg. Now that you've released the steam maybe you could climb down off that thing."

Connor had forgotten that the rod he was standing on was hurting Killeen. He jumped off of it and said.

"Sorry, Mr. Killeen."

"Don't worry none boy. You did it. Now we need to get me and Johnson out of here."

"Yes, sir."

Chapter 15

Connor looked around for something he could use to free Killeen. There was a rod sticking out of the wood spilled into the cab from the tender.

"If I can get this free I think I can use it."

Connor turned and started to struggle with the rod. Pulling at it with all his might.

"Killeen what's going on in there?" a voice from outside shouted. It was the conductor McDougall. "That was a nice job releasing the steam. I thought she was going to blow."

"It was the boy that released the steam. Now he's got to get Johnson and me out," Killeen said.

"We've got the passengers rounded up and everything is under control out here. What can we do to help? None of us can crawl into that cab."

"Start moving the wood away from the tender to make a way into the cab. The boy and I will get me and Johnson free, but we're going to need a way out. Neither one of us can climb out."

Connor had been struggling with the long iron rod while Killeen and McDougall had been talking. He was barely moving it when Jake said.

"Connor if you take some of the wood off the pile I think you can get it out."

"I've got nowhere to put it."

"Hand it to me. I'll throw it away from the train."

Connor climbed onto the pile of wood and began handing Jake the split logs from the wood tender. Jake would grab each heavy log and heave it away from the train. Connor could hear the people working outside the cab on the wood on the other side of the pile. After several minutes of moving the wood, the rod was much more exposed now. Connor grabbed it and gave it a great pull. It barely moved.

"Connor that thing should come out now. Not much is holding it," Jake said.

Connor with one final mighty pull the rod came free. Connor stumbled backward over one of the pieces of wood in a pile holding the rod tightly. He looked down and kicked it, the wood on the floor was making everything harder. That is when the idea hit him. It was something his father had taught him. He dropped the rod and began to stack the logs next to Killeen.

"What are you doing boy?"

"Making a fulcrum just like my father taught me. I'll have you out of there in a minute."

He only had to pile a couple of the logs together so it was high enough that he could use it. Then Connor grabbed the rod and rested it on top of the logs he had stacked on top of one another. Then he slipped the tip of the rod under the handle that was trapping Killeen's leg. Resting the rod on the log would increase his ability to lift or bend something. His dad had told him it was called a fulcrum.

"Boy, that's some good thinking. I'll push up when you start." Killeen asked

"Ok, one, two, three."

Connor pulled down on the rod with all his might. The handle began to move, but it wasn't enough. It wasn't going to work he wasn't strong enough. He had to find another way. He thought for a moment and realized he could use his body weight to apply enough pressure. He made sure the stack of logs was steady enough before he would try. Then Connor jumped up on the rod and laid across it using all of his weight. Slowly the handle began to move.

"That's a boy. Keep it up were almost there."

Finally, with a sudden crack, the handle moved enough that Killeen began to pull his leg out. Connor stayed on the rod until Killeen was able to free his leg. When he crawled out from under the handle, Connor jumped down from the rod.

"Good job boy. Let's see to Johnson. He hasn't made a sound in a while."

Killeen hobbled on one leg, but he and Connor were able to begin to uncover Johnson. He was under more wood from the tender. As they worked, they could hear McDougall and the others working furiously outside. Just as they uncovered Johnson the men from outside broke through into the cab.

McDougall stuck his head through the opening and said.

"Good to see you boys," McDougall said with a smile. "Let's get Killeen out first so we can get at Johnson."

Strong arms reached into the cab and lifted Killeen out. Then Connor helped other men uncover Johnson, he was still alive but bleeding badly from a head wound.

"Come on out Connor," McDougall said. "There's enough room now for a couple of men to get Johnson out."

Connor climbed out of the cab and was startled at what he saw. Most of the passengers were gathered around the cab of the engine and had been helping with the wood. When Connor appeared some of the passengers actually clapped. He looked up and saw Hermann standing there with a big smile on his scared face.

"Nice job Connor."

That was all he said, but it was more than enough. Connor walked away from the crowd and sat down on the ground. He didn't know how long it had been since the train wreck, but he had not stopped since it happened. He was suddenly exhausted. He could barely move. He looked down at his best shirt that he had worn to work, it was dirty and in tatters. His hands were black with grime and dirt and were bleeding from several scratches he had gotten.

Jake came up and sat down beside him. They looked at each other and shook their heads.

"Don't think I want to do that again," Jake said with a smile.

"Nope. Me neither," Connor said. Then gesturing to his ruined shirt and pants, he said. "My Ma is going to kill me."

"Connor you mean to tell me after going through everything we just been through you're scared of what your mother is going to say about your shirt and pants?"

"You don't know my Ma. I'd face a train wreck any day to her being mad at me."

Jake just looked at him then burst out laughing. Soon Connor was laughing just as hard. They laughed so long and hard their sides hurt.

Chapter 16

Connor ran into the house slamming the door behind him. They no longer lived in the tiny shanty by the tracks, they lived in a beautiful home in the neighborhood with the other railroad workers. After the wreck, the railroad hired Connor full time as a Butcher Boy. He had made enough money that with what his mother was now making they could afford to live in a decent house.

"Ma, Ma. I'm running late. I need my box and my shirt. I don't want to be late. It's the first time the whole crew will be back together."

Connor's mother looked up from her ironing board and said.

"Young man you just settle down. You don't come running into this house that way."

"But Ma..."

"You know the rule."

Connor turned around and went back outside. This time he entered the house the way his mother insisted he do. They had been able to buy furniture and a rug or two, so the house was a fine place. His mother kept it spotless and was proud of the home. Connor came back in the front door and closed it properly.

"Ma, I'm running late. I need..."

"I know what you need now just hold your horses."

"It's just that Mr. Killeen and Johnson both will be back, and I don't want to be late."

"It's a miracle they were able to return to work."

Connor knew his mother was right. Killeen's leg had been broken badly, and it had taken longer to heal than expected. He walked with a limp, but he was walking and ready to go back to work. Johnson had been the most seriously injured of the crew, and he had just gotten permission to return to the road again. McDougall the conductor had been working for a couple of weeks now. McDougall insisted that Connor be his butcher boy. He told the station agent he would not leave the station without him.

"I know it's very exciting, but you need to slow down and get ready."

"Is Jake ready yet?" Connor asked.

After the wreck, Jake had helped so many people that McDougall had convinced the station agent to hire him. So Jake got hired as a wiper. He would do the bidding of the engineer and fireman. Jake had been on the job for as long as Connor. When Connor's mother found out he had no parents and how he had helped Connor she had insisted that he stay with them. Jake was giving part of his salary to his mother for room and board. He came out of the bedroom dressed in his new thousand-mile shirt and blue jeans.

"I'm ready Mrs. Galway," Jake said.

"Good. Now run along and help Bridget with Connor's box while he gets dressed."

"Yes, ma'am."

McDougall had allowed Connor to start selling newspapers, candy, cigars, and paperback novels to the passengers. Only the best of the butcher boys were allowed to sell their own goods by a conductor. This brought even more money for his mother and sister. Jake came out of the kitchen carrying a tin box.

"Here you go."

Bridget had filled it with all of his goods, and it was ready for the trip. His mother handed Connor his cleaned and ironed shirt. He put it on and buttoned it up then took his box.

"I'm ready," Connor said.

"Me too," Jake said.

"Now you boys be careful. Do you understand? One train wreck is enough for anybody. You know how I worry."

"Always ma," Connor said.

"Yes, ma'am Mrs. Galway."

"I'll see you at the station before you leave. You're working the noon aren't you?"

"Yes, Ma," Connor said as he and Jake walked out the door.

The station agent had also agreed to let his mother set up a small table where she would sell her baked goods, pickles and sliced meats to the passengers. They were doing just fine, Connor thought.

Connor and Jake walked down the street and headed for the rail yards. They strode along heads held high. They were known in the community after the wreck. They had earned the respect of the other railroad men and their families. Connor knew his father would be proud of him.

They carefully crossed the rail yard looking for the train they were to crew. Connor spotted McDougall standing next to a new engine talking to Killeen. It was terrific to see Killeen up and about.

The company had investigated the wreck and determined that it had not been his fault. It had been a broken wheel on the first baggage car that had derailed the train.

Then Connor saw Johnson stick his head out of the engine's cab and say something to the other two. They all laughed. Johnson looked up and saw Connor and Jake he smiled and waved. McDougall saw the two and pulled out his watch to check the time.

"We're on time Captain," Connor said.

"Yes, yes you are," McDougall said. "Now the best crew on the line is finally back together."

Then everyone was silent for a moment. Connor realized that it was the first time since the wreck they had all been together except for O'Brian. One by one he exchanged glances with each man there. It was an acknowledgment of what they had been through together and the loss of their co-worker.

They had been through the toughest test there was for a train crew and survived. They had saved most of the passengers and gotten them safely to their destinations. Now each time they were together each of them had memories of that night. Those memories would bind them together from this day on.

Connor now knew what it meant to be a railroad man as he stood there among his crew. It wasn't about the clothes or the swagger. It was about the danger and responsibility each carried for the passengers and the other crewmembers. Being a railroad man meant you understood the risks, knew your job and did the best you could every time you climbed onto a train.

McDougall looked at his watch again and said.

"Boys it's time to load up."

Killeen, Johnson, and Jake climbed up into the cab of the engine. McDougall and Connor walked back to the first passenger car. Connor climbed up and stashed his metal box full of his goods for sale then stood on the platform with McDougall. McDougall looked up, and down the train then swung his lantern to signal Killeen.

"All aboard. We've got work to do."

The train began to move. Connor watched as the yard went by and felt the thrill he always felt when a train started on a new trip. He was a real railroad man now.

Chapter 17

Glossary

Brakeman- before automatic air brakes were invented men had to ride on top the cars to apply brakes so the trains could stop. They rode in the open on the roofs day and night no matter what the weather. When brakes were needed they had to jump from one car to another to brake each one. The brakeman would turn a wheel that was connected to the cars wheels to slow the car.

Butcher Boy- a young boy whose job is to walk the aisles of a passenger train offering water to the passengers. He might be allowed to sell snacks and books if he had proven himself to the conductor. Tips from the passengers supplemented his salary.

Call Boy- a young boy that the local station agent would send out to find men to fill out a train crew. He made as much as a dollar for each man he found.

Conductor- the conductor was responsible for all aspects of the train and it's journey. He had to make sure the passenger's luggage was on board. It up to him to make sure any freight the train carried was properly stored. He took the passengers tickets and collected their fares. He made sure the train was on time and made the proper stops. With all of these responsibilities many passengers and crew referred to him as the Captain.

Engineer- the engineer drove the train. He had to monitor the steam pressure, the speed, the track ahead, and many other things to keep the train moving and on time. He was constantly adjusting the throttle to go up and down hills or navigate curves. Engineers were assigned a specific engine and no other engineer could touch it.

Fireman- the fireman was responsible stoking the fire in firebox that heated the water that created the steam to run the train. He had to be strong because he might shovel tons of coal or wood during the course of a trip.

Train Wrecks- train wrecks were not uncommon in the late 1880's. The railroads were expanding so fast that safety was sometimes not their first concern. There were many causes of train wrecks from equipment failure to mistakes in scheduling. Derailments could be caused by equipment failure as in this story or deliberate acts by bandits. Robbers would remove a rail so the train would wreck and they could rob the passengers and the train. There were head on collisions and rear end collisions caused by scheduling mistakes by the train masters. Bridges would collapse because of floods or poor construction. There were boiler explosions when something went wrong with engine. There were runaway trains caused by brake failure or the crew not setting the brakes properly. The railroads were a brand new technology and there was much to learn about their construction and operations. So working on the railroad was a dangerous and exciting occupation.

Made in the USA
Middletown, DE
02 January 2020